The Wishing Stone

by Steve Smallman

Illustrated by Rebecca Elliott

NEW BURLINGTON BOOKS

Armadillo lived in the swamp.

He was lonely and wished that
he could find a friend.

But whenever anyone came near him,
he would roll himself up into a ball
and keep very still until they went away.

"What should we play today," squeaked Mouse. "Hide-and-seek?"

"No, I always lose," grumbled Flamingo.

"I know... **WATER FIGHT!**" shouted Monkey, and he pushed Flamingo into the swamp and jumped in after her.

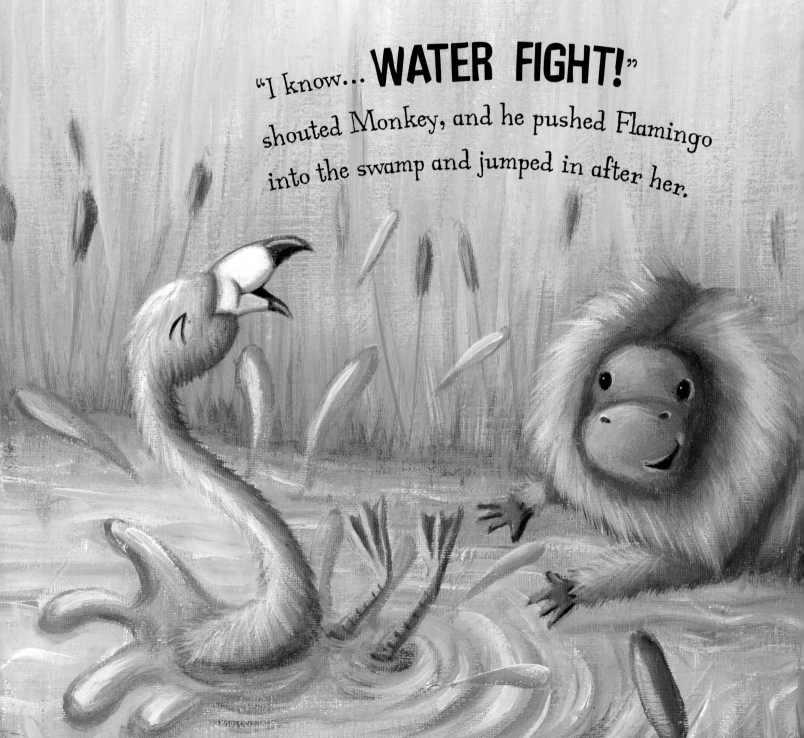

Mouse couldn't swim, so he sat down
grumpily on a funny-looking stone.

"I wish I had a wading pool so
I could play, too," he said quietly.

That night, Armadillo
got to work.

Using his strong claws,
he dug a wide hole and
filled it with water.

Then, tired out, he rolled up
into a ball and went to sleep.

"A wading pool!' squeaked
Mouse excitedly the next morning.

"My wish came true.
That stone must be magic!"

"Let me try," said Flamingo, sitting on the stone. "I wish we had a secret den," she said.

"You'll have to wait until tomorrow for it to work," said Mouse.

That night, Armadillo
worked hard.

He cut down branches and
gathered leaves, and by the time
the sun started to rise, he had
made a wonderful secret den.

Tired out, he rolled up into
a ball and went to sleep.

"The wishing stone worked!"
squawked Flamingo the next day,
climbing inside the secret den.

"My turn!" cried Monkey,
sitting on the stone. "I wish
there was some food in here!"

"That's a stupid wish," said Flamingo.

"Not if you're hungry," said Monkey.

"But you'll have to wait until tomorrow
for it to work," said Mouse.

Armadillo liked
to eat bugs.

So that night, he dug a hole inside the den,
lined it with leaves, and then filled it with all
the tastiest-looking bugs he could find.

Then, tired out, he rolled up
into a ball and went to sleep.

"Yuck!" Monkey, Flamingo, and Mouse didn't like bugs.

"That wishing stone is useless!" shouted Monkey, and kicked it toward the deepest part of the swamp.

"HELP!" cried Armadillo, as he rolled faster and faster. "I can't swim!" SPLASH!

"The wishing stone talks," gasped Mouse.
"And it can't swim!"

Monkey found a big stick and pushed it
into the water.

Armadillo grabbed it, and the three friends
pulled with all their strength until...

PLOP!

Out came Armadillo, soggy and gasping for breath.

"Did you make my wading pool?" asked Mouse.

"And our den?" added Flamingo. Armadillo nodded.

"What about the bugs?" asked Monkey.

"They're my favorite," sniffed Armadillo.
"I thought you would like them, too."

"Thank you. You're very kind," they replied, smiling.

Mouse, Flamingo, Monkey, and Armadillo
soon became best friends.

With Monkey's help, Armadillo learned to swim.
He even let Mouse ride on his back
in the deep end.

"Maybe wishes do come true,"
Armadillo thought happily.

Notes for parents and teachers

- Look at the front cover of the book together. Can the children guess what the story might be about? Read the title together. Does this give them more of a clue or make it more confusing?

- What words could the children use to describe the armadillo?

- Why is he so kind to the other animals? Are they kind to him? Ask the children to talk about someone they are kind to. Who is kind to them? Why is kindness important?

- Armadillos like to eat bugs. What do the children think the other animals like to eat? Ask the children to draw pictures of their favorite foods.

- At the end of the story, Armadillo thinks that wishes do come true. Can the children remember what he wished for at the beginning of the story? If the children could make a wish, what would they wish for, and why?

- Discuss what it feels like to be lonely or "left out," and talk about different ways to make friends. Talk about why it's also important to include new friends.

A NEW BURLINGTON BOOK
The Old Brewery
6 Blundell Street
London N7 9BH

Copyright © QEB Publishing, Inc.
2010

Published in the United States by
QEB Publishing, Inc
3 Wrigley, Suite A
Irvine, CA 92618

www.qed-publishing.co.uk

ISBN 978 1 78171 267 2

Printed in China

A CIP record for this book is available from the Library of Congress.

Editor: Amanda Askew
Designers: Vida and Luke Kelly